Dawning Desire

Jax Wilder

Dawning Desire© 2024 by Jax Wilder
Rainbow Quartz Publishing

COVER ART BY RAINBOW QUARTZ PUBLISHING
IG: RAINBOW QUARTZ PUBLISHING

HTTPS://RQPUBLISHING.COM/
HTTPS://AUTHORJAXWILDER.COM

ISBN: 978-1-961714-18-2

1
Tai-Yang

The old gods were cruel.

Once fate is written, it must be obeyed. Fate is, after all, required by the stars. I wanted to please the gods, find my place in the universe, and follow the prophecy as it was written.

Then I met her. I didn't want to fall in love with her, but she made it impossible not to.

I was born Tai-Yang, goddess of the sun. I was destined to marry Hou Yi, the famed archer of the sky. The Earth was being bombarded by ten suns. Had it continued, the Earth would scorch—no plants, no animals, no life. The oceans would dry up, and the Earth would have become a comatose molten ball of iron forever. Hou Yi was a champion of Earth. He shot down nine of ten suns, leaving just one—my sun and namesake. This sun provides light and heat for the planet to thrive. The oceans flourished, animal and plant life evolved, and Hou Yi was touted as a hero. For his bravery, he was given the elixir of immortality.

We were a literal match made in the heavens—a hero of Earth and the goddess of the last sun. Our first courting was shortly after Hou Yi received the elixir. He decided not to drink it immediately. He was handsome and intelligent, and he had a huge heart. I gave the relationship my all. It was fate. We attended banquets together, which seemed to please the gods, for a time. I could make it work. I would smile and say all the right things, and we could live as it was written. At the Celestial Promenade, we danced all night. Hou Yi held me close, looking intensely into my eyes. I gazed deep within his soul. He was always an admirable man.

In many fated romances, the men are terrible. Heroes rarely make good lovers. They tend to fall into a state of post-achievement blues, unsure of where to go next. But I didn't see that path in Hou Yi. All I saw was an extremely passionate man who wanted to be in love, work at love, and stay in love. I was lucky in that way.

After a few spins around the dance floor, I took a break to grab a glass of wine.

"Let me get that for you," Hou Yi said.

"Thank you, but I need a short reprieve to catch my breath. I'll be back," I said before parting ways. I found the bartender and requested a glass of red.

"That's quite the handsome guy on your arm tonight," a woman said at the bar.

"Thank you. That is Hou Yi, the archer who—"

"Shot down the nine suns. I know. I don't think a single person here doesn't know who Hou Yi is. Or Tai-Yang, for that matter," she said with a cheeky smile.

When I found her eyes, I lost all thought. She was stunning. A vision of ethereal beauty, radiating an otherworldly aura that captivated me the second I saw her. Her presence evoked a sense of tranquility. With skin as luminous as the moon itself, she possessed a glow that lit up the night sky. Like pools of silver, her eyes shimmered with ancient wisdom and the secrets of the cosmos. They had speckles that looked like dancing stars. I was so stricken that I forgot I was pouring wine and spilled it all over my cup. She laughed.

"Oh, stars," I said, pulling back the pitcher to stop the flow. I set down the goblet and asked the bartender for a napkin.

She was already on it, handing me a towel. As I dabbed the mess all over the back of my hand, I looked down and saw that she was already wiping up the floor.

"Oh, I'm sure someone else can do that. Really, you don't have to do that," I said.

"It's okay. It's no big deal, I'm already down here," she said.

When I finished wiping my hands, I bent down and helped her.

"Thank you. I am so embarrassed," I said.

"Don't be. Accidents happen, and I don't mind pitching in to help." She looked into my eyes, and my whole body tingled. Cascading waves of silver and blue hair tumbled down her back like shimmering strands of moonbeams, framing a face of unparalleled grace and serenity. Never in my life had I been so struck by someone. I knew in that moment this woman was my match. I had to know her. I needed to be near her.

I watched her return the towel. She was adorned with robes woven from the fabric of the night sky. She moved with a grace and elegance that mirrored the silent power of celestial bodies. She returned to me and handed me a damp towel infused with rose petals to wipe my hands. I reached for the towel, but she took control. She wiped the top of my right hand, flipped it over, and tenderly wiped my palm. She repeated this motion on my left hand, and butterflies took flight inside me. She wiped her hands with the towel and then walked away to dispose of it.

I grabbed my overfilled wine and carefully sipped at the top until I could more easily hold it. I looked back to where the magical woman was standing. She was gone. I walked the room but was unable to locate her again. Disappointed, I made my way back to the bar, thinking that maybe she had returned. Hou Yi was standing at the bar waiting for me.

"There you are," he said.

I smiled weakly. "Here I am."

"I worried you lost your way," he said genuinely.

"Ha, no, no. I overpoured my wine and made a mess of everything," I said, fumbling over my words. "A woman rescued me. I was just looking to thank her, but she's disappeared." I left out some of the finer details, of course.

Hou Yi poured himself a goblet. "That was nice of her," he said. "Who was she?"

"I don't know. After she took the dirty towels away, I lost track of her and didn't catch her name," I explained.

"That's too bad. I'm sure we'll run into her again," Hou Yi said, taking my hand.

"I hope so," I smiled to myself.

The music changed to a waltz.

"May I have this dance?" Hou Yi asked.

I am a sucker for a waltz, so I downed the remainder of my goblet of wine, slammed it down on the bar counter, and smiled. "Let's do this."

Hou Yi cleared a full goblet, took my hand, and led me back toward the floor. The enchanting melody pulled us onto the dance floor. My hand in Hou Yi's, we began our dance, fluid and poised. Dancing the waltz is like being swept away in a graceful whirlwind of elegance and romance. Desire and sophistication emanate from my pores. I don't just feel sexy. I am sexy.

I glanced at the other dancers and saw a flash of indigo. I twirled around for a second look, and there, dancing with an unknown man, was the luminescent goddess herself.

"There she is," I said, probably a little too loudly.

"Huh?" Hou Yi struggled to talk over the music.

One, two, three. We continued moving to the music. One, two, three.

"There. That's the woman who helped me with the wine spill."

"Oh, Luna?" Hou Yi asked.

"Luna? Like, Luna? The goddess of the Moon Luna?" I was stunned.

At some point, I stopped dancing, which threw off the others waltzing in beat. Everyone was staring at me; all I could think of was Luna. Was she watching me, too? Hou Yi pulled me off the dance floor.

He laughed a little uncomfortably, "Are you okay?"

"Yes," I said, unable to take my eyes off Luna. The sun and the moon. Everything suddenly made perfect sense. The rest was, well, history.

"Would you get me a glass of water?" I rested my hand on Hou Yi.

"Sure, darling," Hou Yi replied.

When he left, Luna came over. "Hello again," she said.

"Hi," I breathed. "I was really hoping to see you again."

"Same, Tai-Yang. Same," Luna's cheeks flushed pink.

"I was wondering if you wanted to come for tea tomorrow?"

"Yes," Luna cleared her throat. "Yes, that would be lovely."

Hou Yi was back with water.

"Thank you," I said, taking the glass.

That was all it took. Our affair began in secret, at first. Hou Yi could tell I was distant. He asked me more than once if this was what I wanted. If he was what I wanted. Every time I said yes, it felt more like a lie. I lied to spare his feelings.

In the end, I had to admit that I was. I bided my time devising a plan. Luna and I spent months discussing how we would spend our lives together. In time, my fear of disappointing the gods faded. I found the courage to tell Hou Yi. He was waiting for me when I got home that day.

"Can we talk?" I asked.

He led me to the sofa. "What's on your mind?"

"I have something to tell you," I said, voice wobbly.

"You're in love with someone else," Hou Yi held my gaze. He was a brilliant man. "I understand. Luna is a lovely woman, and I wish you both every happiness." I lunged forward, fighting back the tears that welled in my eyes, and hugged him. I held Hou Yi tightly as I sobbed.

"It's okay," he whispered.

"I'm scared to tell the gods." My voice cracked. His kindness cut deeper than anger ever could.

"I will come with you and stand witness to your side," Hou Yi said.

This made me cry even harder. How lucky was I to find two such amazing people in this world?

Not lucky enough. The gods were not only displeased with my announcement, they were angry. They made it clear that Hou Yi and I were fated to be with one another. It was impossible to deny the prophecy. I told them Hou Yi was in no way responsible for my choices. I shifted my focus from him. He deserved nothing from their divine contempt. I stepped forward and took full responsibility for my actions. I stood firm in my belief that I would be with Luna and not Hou Yi. They spared Hou Yi. They did not spare me.

The gods proclaimed that I would be alone. Luna was banished to live on Earth as a mortal for ten thousand years. She would reincarnate over and over until her time was served. Luna would live these lives with no memory of her life as a goddess. Worse than that, she would have no memories of me. Through thick tears, I fell to my knees and begged the court of gods. One of the gods took pity on me.

"Since you are the goddess of the sun and she the goddess of the moon, I shall grant you a single kindness. When the Earth eclipses the moon over the cnidarian embayment, and only when Luna is in that location, she will remember everything. She will remember she is the moon goddess. She will know what has happened, and she will know of you, Tai-Yang."

I broke into a sob. "Thank you," I cried.

"Temporarily," she said. "At that time, Luna will remain for only twelve Earth hours, then she will fade away once more."

It was then I realized this was no mercy. This was another way to torture me.

2
Ophelia

"Hey you, I thought you were going on vacation?" Melody asked.

I gazed up from my computer. "No, that's next week. Hopefully, anyway. I have to get through this deposition tonight so we can formally be done with discovery and petition for a trial date. With the current backlog, I think the court will grant me enough time to take a weekend off."

"You know this office has twenty other attorneys to take over that case, right?" Melody said.

"Yes, but when I take on a case, I like to see it through as much as I can," I said.

I am trying to make partner. Melody probably knows that, but I wouldn't say it out loud. I am positive all the paralegals are current on the latest office intrigue. Either way, there are some cards I like to hold close to my chest.

"You need to rest. You work too much. I promise you're like the top lawyer at this firm by a landslide. You can take a break," Melody said.

"That's very sweet of you," I said before returning to my monitor.

Dawning Desire

Ever since I was a child, I was driven. You might assume I had strict parents who pushed me toward this level of success. But, I was always intrinsically driven. In elementary school, I was flagged for the gifted and talented program. In middle school, I was put on the advanced placement program. By high school, I was taking college courses. I graduated with my high school diploma and an associate degree in criminal justice from the local community college.

One of my professors in college was a retired attorney. He told his firm about me. After an application and interview process, fast forward one year, and I was awarded a full-ride scholarship to law school. After law school, I interned at my professor's old firm. After passing the bar, I worked my way up and was offered a full-time position. I worked at that firm for years before getting a generous offer at my current firm. This job nearly tripled my income and offered me a path to my ultimate goal: making partner.

Melody has been my paralegal for a few years now. Our firm handles a wide variety of law, but my specialty is criminal law. Melody probably knows me better than anyone. I see her more than my own family. On more than one occasion, Melody has said, "You need to go on a date." Or, "I know a great guy. What's your type?" Or, "When was the last time you went out with anyone?"

I've been out with men, okay. I had a high school sweetheart. We went to prom. I had sex in the back of his Mustang. I did the normal teenage things, but my only true satisfaction was feeding my drive. I love to work. I love being good at work. I love being the best. I dated in college. College men make the absolute worst boyfriends. Many of them were living on their own for the first time. This also meant drinking alcohol, wanting to party, and sampling the buffet of life.

I tried. Really, I did. I wanted to let my freak flag fly. I even smoked pot at a rush party one night. All the college boys were a letdown. It wasn't their fault. We were just in different places. In my adult life, I find dating a waste of energy. Whenever I think I've found a similarly driven man who understands me, and that I'm attracted to, he would eventually succumb to feelings of emasculation. It is not my responsibility to nurse their inferiority complex and bend to the patriarchy. If you can't handle a powerful woman, you can't handle me.

"You inspire me," Melody said.

I pulled down my reading glasses and peered over the top at her. "Really? I inspire you?"

"Yeah. Last weekend, I went out with this guy. Met him on the apps. He was so funny, outgoing, and charming in his profile, I thought, why not?" Melody said.

"They usually are," I laughed. I set down my paperwork and shed my glasses altogether.

"We talked about jobs pretty much right away. He's a project manager for some software company. I don't really know. I didn't understand half the words he used." Melody was always very dramatic with her tales. She talks with her hands. Melody wiped away at nothing. "I told him that I was a paralegal at this top law firm and was also working towards finishing law school so that I could become an attorney. Telling him it would be my dream to start my own firm one day."

"Okay. And?" I asked.

"He was initially like, wow, that's awesome when I told him I was a paralegal. Then, once I had explained that I was driven and had goals, it was like, oh no, a woman can't have dreams that aren't having babies and being a wife," Melody waved her arms up and down, pacing like a caveman.

I just laughed.

"He was such a misogynistic asshole out of nowhere. I just left his ass at the bar and went home."

"I fail to see how I was the inspiration here," I smiled gently.

"Oh! Normally, I would have gone home and cried myself into a tub of Ben and Jerry's. Instead of feeling like I did something wrong, I thought of you." Melody smiled.

"Me?" I arched a brow.

"Yeah! I thought, what would Ophelia do? Ophelia would have given that dude an earful, gone home to her penthouse apartment, drawn herself a bath, had a glass of wine, and enjoyed everything she got all by herself."

"Oh yeah? That's what I'd do?"

"Well, the inspiring part is that you have all those things and didn't need anyone's help. I don't need a man to buy it for me. If I find a man, he will be an addition to my life, not a hindrance. And he sure as hell won't be my whole life," Melody stood on the chair, arms stretched to the sky like Norma Rae.

"You go, girl," I raised a fist to the sky.

"We are going to find men who can handle strong, independent women. Men who are true feminists and aren't afraid to scream it from the rooftops. Men who lift their women, not tie them down," Melody raised her fists to the sky in kind.

"Here, here!" I shouted, and together we punched the sky.

The truth is, I did believe that men like that could exist. One of the partners is married to one. When I first met him at the office party, I was blown away by his presence. He was a tall, burly, hairy man. He looked like a lumberjack. To me, he epitomized what societal norms dictate a man should look like. When his wife gave her speech to the entire firm, I couldn't look away from him, and he couldn't look away from her. He was beaming at her every word, tears in his eyes. When her speech was over, he clapped the loudest. Melody and I gossiped about him for weeks after.

I asked once if they ever fought.

"Of course, we fight! We fight over the dumbest stuff. Kids, money, etc. He knows exactly what to say to get on every one of my nerves. However, at the end of the day, there isn't anyone I would rather have on my nerves than that man," she said.

I believed her wholeheartedly. It's funny how one person and one great story can inspire hope. I made sure to tell Melody about that conversation, too. I really do hope she finds a partner like that one day.

There is, of course, no hope for me.

3
Lea

"What is that?" I asked.

Park, my faithful employee, stumbled into the bookshop with a gigantic cardboard box. "These are the supplies for the Mooncake Festival," Park said, plopping the heavy box onto the floor with a loud thud.

Fall in Coral Cove is unlike any place in the world. The second wave of tourism dies down temporarily at the end of August. It gears up for the third wave in late October, right before the holidays. The crisp sea air rolls in, driving the multicolored leaves from their branches. This shifts the taste and smell of the air. I'm filled with a sense of excitement riding on mystical energy. The boats roll in for the Wooden Boat Festival, which usually kicks off the fall season.

The Mooncake Festival is the 15th day of the 8th month in the Chinese lunar calendar. This year, that falls in early September of our Gregorian calendar, making this the early kick-off festival in the fall instead of the Wooden Boat Festival. Pair such an exciting holiday with a lunar eclipse, and you can't help but feel the static in the air surrounding the town.

"What kind of supplies do you need?" I asked. "I thought it was just a viewing party for the lunar eclipse?"

"Well, yeah. However, there is a whole festival surrounding it, too. I thought we could string up a lantern display in the front window. I got a cute Chinese dragon marionette that we can hang," Park said. He pulled out the puppet and set it on the counter. "I've also got some window-cling stars and a moon."

"Oh, those are pretty!" I said. "What's all of this?" I pointed to the bottom of the box, filled with smaller individual boxes.

"Those are mooncakes. They're a little pastry, usually filled with a savory middle. Still, I had May over at Golden Chopsticks make them with a custard filling," Park said. He held one up so I could see inside.

I took the box from his hand and inspected it closer. "I think I need to play quality control on this one," I said, popping the entire confection into my mouth in one bite.

"Oh my stars, that is delicious," I said while chewing. The exterior was buttery, flaky, and perfectly balanced to the creamy interior. It would take a lot of strength to not eat them all in one sitting. I swallowed the rest. "I'm going to have to take one of these home to Alex. We might have to double that number for us. You know Alex is a sweet man."

"Ha. I already put a few in the car for Ben," Park beamed.

We are too alike sometimes.

"What's the plan with these, then? Are we selling them?" I asked. "We might need a food handler's permit for that."

"No, I was thinking a free gift with purchase kind of a promotion," Park said. "I am fairly confident we can get around the food permit that way."

"I think you're right. People can decline them that way, and no one paid for them," I said confidently. "Great idea."

"Thank you," Park said.

"Should we decorate now?" I asked.

"Yeah, why not? Mooncake Festival is next weekend," Park said, grabbing the bags off the counter. I moved the box upstairs to the office.

A breeze blew through the bookstore. I looked over at the door. It was closed, and no one entered. None of the front windows are open. I looked around, and I was hit with a crazy sensation. A familiar sensation.

"Park," I said with a cheesy smirk.

Park turned to me. "Uh oh, what?" he said.

"I just felt it. There's holiday magic brewing," I winked.

Park smiled. "I love me some holiday magic."

4
Ophelia

I finished reviewing the final deposition for the third time. Feeling confident that I had pulled out all the relevant pieces, I filed my pre-trial dismissal motion. My client has a solid alibi; the testimony of the eyewitnesses all shed doubt on the suspect being my client, and yet, part of me still thinks this is going to trial. The prosecuting attorney has already tried to dangle an unflattering plea deal. He seemed confident they have a case against my client.

I'm going to destroy them.

I laughed to myself as my boss entered my office.

"What are you still doing here?" he asked.

"What do you mean?" I was seriously confused by the question. It was only 6 p.m., and discovery was nearly over.

"You've already filed your motion for dismissal. Go home! Relax. It's Friday night. You're not going to hear back until Monday."

He wasn't wrong.

"I know, but it's going to be denied. We're going to go to trial," I said.

"Probably, but I'm sure you've heard about Judge Ashworth?" he said.

"No, what happened?"

"He had a heart attack." He waved my initial shock away. "He's fine. Well, he's going to be fine. He had to have an emergency bypass and will be out for a while. Judge Payne has to shift her workload and take on some of Ashworth's cases. All of our non-violent offenses have been put on backlog."

"Oh. When did that happen?" I was stunned that Melody hadn't messaged me. I grabbed my phone and looked to be sure.

"Yesterday evening. There was an email."

"I am behind on my emails today because I was combing through those last deposition questions. I'm sorry," I said.

"Don't apologize. You can rest easy this weekend."

"That sounds like me, doesn't it? Resting easy?" I laughed.

My boss turned to leave my office, but I stopped him before he could grab the handle of the door.

"Actually, sir. This allows me to take on that Johnson case I gave to Randall," I said.

"Ophelia," he said, staring at me.

"Yes?" I said, breaking the uncomfortable pause.

"You need a break. This whole situation has come at an opportune moment. Weren't you going on vacation at the end of next week?" He walked over and sat down in my visitor's chair.

"Well, kind of. I was going to go away just for the weekend."

"Extend it. Take a full week," Timothy said.

I felt a pinch in my stomach. This was not a good sign for making partner.

"I need the partners to understand that I am in it to win it," I said.

"Ophelia. No one at this firm works harder than you. The partners all know that," he explained.

"I can take on more," I said.

"No. The partners need to see you taking care of yourself, too. I have been here many years and have seen many attorneys kill themselves, bending over backward and taking on too much, trying to impress the partners. Do you know where it landed them? In burnout."

"But..." I didn't know what else to say.

"Connect with Judge Payne, and then take a week off. Show the partners upstairs that you know how to refill your cup," he said.

"Sorry?" I scrunched my face.

"Your cup. You know the old expression. You can't fill from an empty cup. A good attorney knows we need a good work-life balance." My boss leaned back in my chair.

"Oh, right. Okay," I said. "I'll submit the paperwork."

"Approved! Where were you going again?"

"Uhm, I was thinking of this small town called Coral Cove," I said.

"Oh, romantic. Are you going with a special someone?" he asked.

"No," I didn't mean to sound as appalled as I came off. "I mean, no. I love the sea and booked a little hotel on the water. The balcony leads right out to the beach. I love watching the tides."

"That sounds perfect," My boss smiled. "I think there's supposed to be an extreme low tide associated with the eclipse too."

I didn't really know what to say. I didn't know my boss kept up with tidal conditions. This is also the first time I have heard about an eclipse.

"There's an eclipse?" I asked.

"I think so. My wife loves Coral Cove, and we get email blasts about the festivals. I saw that there is an eclipse festival. Moon something festival," he explained.

"And the tides?" I asked.

"What can I say? I'm a nerd. Plus, you know what controls them?"

"The tides?" I asked.

"The moon."

5
Lillian

The forthcoming eclipse here in Coral Cove fills me with emotion. Every inch of me is vibrating. Every one of my favorite memories is here. Every adventure, all the pieces of my heart, and everything worth living for have always been here. But there is a sadness that slowly creeps in at the edges. It's like a ticking clock, knowing everything is fleeting. There's a limit on happiness and how much I can have. Despite knowing how amazing my time will be, I pre-mourn leaving. It's a complex emotion to describe—the loss I know will come following the purest joy I will ever know. There's an anxiety underlying my happiest emotions. What if she doesn't come? What if I have to wait two and a half more years until I see her again? Will I find the love of my life in this little town?

I pulled up the familiar driveway to my little purple house. I closed my eyes and inhaled the salty, sweet sea air. I sucked in a few breaths before heading inside.

"Hello, Elenore? I brought you coffee from Joe's," I said to the empty kitchen. I set the coffee and breakfast burritos down on the counter. "El, if you don't get your pretty little ass out here, I'm going to eat your breakfast and spit in your coffee."

"Don't you dare," Elenore said, popping out of the stairwell.

"Oh, there you are," I said, licking the side of her coffee cup and handing it over.

"You're incorrigible," Elenore said, taking the coffee. "Are you going to the Mooncake Festival?"

"Uhm, maybe?" I said. "I need to stop by The Sunflower and make a last-minute bouquet for Alex. Apparently, he's surprising Lea, and between you and me, I'm not about to piss off Mr. Clause," I winked.

"Oh man, not you too? Poor guy can't catch a break," Elenore grinned.

"Hey, I'm just saying. On the off chance Alex is Santa, I'm not about to say I don't believe in fairies," I said. "You feel me?"

Elenore burst into a belly-grabbing giggle. "I'm telling him you said so!"

"I dare you," I said with a smile. "Later, I'm supposed to meet someone for the lunar eclipse. If we cross paths with the festival, it's a possibility. What about yourself?"

Elenore smiled sweetly. "I'll be at the Neptune all day. Pray that a tall, cute, rugged drink of water comes in and sweeps me off my feet?"

"Oh sure, why not," I said, unwrapping my breakfast and taking a bite.

Today would be a great day. I can feel it.

6
Ophelia

My plane landed with a thud. A few people yelped. I finished my book. It felt wrong, like I was breaking the law somehow, but I took the week to retreat to Coral Cove. To ease my mind, I brought my work laptop. I checked several times that I had the charger as well. I felt uneasy the entire flight and drive to Coral Cove. I called my secretary and checked in twice before I made it to my bed and breakfast.

When I got checked in, I eased a bit. It was the cutest space I had ever rented, nestled above a Chinese restaurant. The smells wafting up were intoxicating and, thankfully, not overpowering. When I opened the door, I was greeted by a small hallway with a shoe rack and coat closet. It was sparse yet sophisticated and in a coastal theme. Absent were the gaudy seashells, paintings of seagulls, and thick ropes. Instead, the room was light and airy, the walls painted with the blue of a calm sea. Two large paintings of mermaid figureheads on a wooden ship hung side by side over the bed. The figureheads were breathtaking.

The mermaid on the right was perched with her arms up, ready to dive into the sea. Her hair wove around and framed her delicate features, dipping down her chest to her supple, exposed breasts. Her tail coiled around the front of the ship. It was tough to decipher where the boat ended, and her tail began. The left mermaid was more stoic. Her hands were poised at the top of her tail along her hips. Her hair was in a messy bun, a few strands blew in the wind, circling her lovely face. Her breasts were perky, similar to her counterpart. They were majestic. I giggled at the thought of them watching over me as I slept.

Underneath them was the most comfortable-looking bed I had ever seen. It was a four-poster without a canopy. The posts were a simple design, and they fit seamlessly into the minimalistic design of the room. The white duvet ruffled the length of the queen-sized bed. It was a cloud. At the head of the bed was a massive sampling of white pillows with varying firmness. A floor-to-ceiling mirror adorned the right side of the bed. Next to that was a small vanity, complete with a ring-light mirror. Nice.

The balcony was directly above the restaurant, and the view overlooked the main street. The balcony was adorned with a wrought iron table and chairs. A small hallway led to a tiny kitchen next to the TV on the wall. The appliances were all a brilliant, almost teal blue. The best part of all was the jetted bathtub. It was gigantic. I could fit three of me inside. I would most definitely be taking a bubble bath or ten.

I needed a bottle of wine first. I slipped my shoes on again and tucked out the door. On the street, I started walking, looking around at what was nearby. Two blocks up the road was a bookstore. "I'll be hitting that up tomorrow." In the distance, I saw what appeared to be a large drawing of a wine bottle. I walked towards it like a moth to a flame. Success! The Winedown.

Walking in, I smiled at the clerk. "Clever wordplay," I said.

"Thank you. It was the wife's idea. She is much more intelligent than I ever was," the older man said.

"Does that make you the owner of this fine establishment?" I asked.

"Yes indeed, young lady. Been here over fifty years," he beamed with pride. "What can I help you find?"

"I'd love a good Malbec," I beamed. "One to go with a bubble bath."

"I've got just the thing." He rang me up and handed me some Argentinian Malbec that I had never heard of. He told me that it had a 96 on the wine score. I'm not much of a connoisseur of wine, but I happily took his word for it.

Back at the bed and breakfast, I ran the water for the tub, making it extra hot. I grabbed a wine glass from the kitchen. A generous pour later, I returned to the bathroom, bottle in hand. The light switch had a dimmer on it, which I promptly lowered. On the counter next to the sink, I found an assortment of candles, scented beads with glass dishes, and bath bombs. I carefully arranged the candles and a couple of the glass bowls around the tub, filling the air with the scent of lavender. I was sure to grab my small black pouch and set it near the tub.

Disrobing, I entered the steaming bath. The hot water shocked my system. I pulled my feet out instinctively before slowly dipping my legs in. I sat my bare bottom on the edge of the porcelain tub. It cooled my nethers; a juxtaposition to the hot water. Feeling confident I could handle the new, cooler temperature, I slipped inside. The warm water enveloped my body in a hug. My back pressed up against the edge of the tub. I grabbed a towel, rolled it up tightly, and placed it behind my head. I took a few sips of my wine, impressed by the soft and subtle flavors, not too sweet or dry. I returned the glass to the edge of the tub. The aroma of wine lingered on my lips, and the lavender potpourri filled the gaps.

I scooched my bottom back and forth to loosen my skin from the bottom of the tub. The warmth of the water replaced the coolness of the porcelain. I leaned back and arched my back. A few cracks in my spine released some tension, and a rush of sensual arousal moved from my chest and down to my feet. I leaned back and glanced down at my cleavage poking out from under the water. My nipples were at attention. I scooped up a handful of water and slowly let it drop onto my chest. The warm water droplets tickled and warmed. I scooped up more and made a swirling pattern on my left breast with my finger. I gently rubbed up against my curves, and another subtle wave of arousal moved into my belly. I let my fingers outline my nipples. I started at the base and worked my way around toward the peaks. I cupped my breasts, feeling the weight of them in my hands, letting them gently bounce in the water. Fingering slow and soft circles around my belly, I closed my eyes. I thought of the mermaids hanging over the bed, watching me. The one with the large, supple breasts was swimming through my thoughts. Her strength and strands of hair billowing.

My hands moved down my belly, deeper to my center. I reached out to the mermaid and softly moved her hair behind an ear, running my fingers down her chin. I leaned in and kissed her gently on the neck, licking my way to her ear. My hands moved rhythmically against my clit.

Fast... slow... fast... slow...

She's here with me now. I've licked and sucked my way down her chest and found the soft and supple breasts of a goddess. I licked my lips. Slowly, to enjoy every moment, I took one of her nipples into my mouth and sucked. I bit a little and flicked with my tongue at her tips. She let out a moan and ran her fingers through my hair, grabbing firmly at the roots. Finding just the right pleasure point.

Fast... fast... slow... fast... fast... slow...

She lifted my chin to meet her mouth and trailed kisses down my body. She paused only momentarily at my breasts, licking them before continuing down my belly. She spread my legs, exposing me to the world. We're on the deck of a boat now. The firm wood beneath my bottom. She pulled me forward so she could see all of me. I reached for my black bag without opening my eyes. I pulled out my toy, sitting in the tub next to me. The mermaid kissed me more firmly, moving down my thigh. She nibbled along the inside of my thigh, lifting one leg and kissing the back of my knees.

"Such beautiful legs. But I want to see what they're hiding," she said coyly, moving her way back up to my center. She slowly moved her fingers along my folds, leaned down, and kissed my folds, slowly opening me with her fingers. She parted her lips and licked at my clit. Every hungry movement brought me closer to the edge. She licked around my nub, teasing me before sucking on it. She released, licking, and then she was sucking harder. The pressure built.

Fast... slow... fast... slow... harder... faster...

The pressure built in my center. I was holding my breath. It only came in short bursts now.

"Come for me, baby," she said firmly. The electricity moved through my chest.

"I want to watch you." I was almost there. I slipped fingers inside of me, never letting up the pressure on my clit.

"Show me." Fireworks exploded behind my eyelids. Bolts of lightning moved through my body. From my clit to the tips of my toes. I kept touching myself, moving circles around my nub. Riding the waves of pleasure that emanated through my whole body.

"Do you want to come again?" she asked.

"Yes. Please, let me come again." I reached for my favorite toy. The silicone had had time to warm in the water next to me.

"I'm going to make you come until you beg me to stop." Butterflies hatched in my belly with anticipation. I released my throbbing clit. I slipped my cock into the tub, letting it find my apex. She slipped her fingers inside of me. I arched my back with pleasure. Slow at first, she moved inside of me slowly, finding a rhythm. My slick slit took all of her. My breath caught, feeling the full girth of her fingers inside of me. She held me there, tasting me.

"You're a snack, baby, absolutely delicious." She thrust inside of me again, over and over.

In. Out. In. Out. The pleasure built deep within me this time. It was an earthquake starting in my core. The waves of pleasure had me breathless.

"That's it, come for me, baby. Come in my mouth. I want to taste your sweet juices."

Oh gods. Oh gods! Oh gods above! A ripple of pleasure ripped through my core. I yelled my gratification to the stars above. My body arched out and then collapsed in on itself as wave after satisfying wave moved through me. Every inch of my body vibrated with pleasure. I froze, remembering the jets in the tub. I clicked the button, and the tub roared to life. I let the jets massage my entire body. I started with my neck.

"Does that feel good, baby?" she whispered in my ear.

I moaned. The jet moved to the middle of my back, relaxing me deeper.

"Do you like it harder?" she asked.

I turned to my side, letting the jet focus on my hip, then all the way to my belly.

"I want to watch you come one more time, baby."

I nodded my agreement. I spread my legs for her, letting the jet find my swollen bud. I lifted one leg out of the water to maneuver as close as possible to the jet. I grabbed my cock and closed my eyes.

"I'm going to make you scream." She entered me again, moving in and out. Thrusting into me, harder and harder. I could feel the warmth building in my center again. This time, my clit and my pussy got the attention they deserved. I thrust, the pressure of the water bringing me almost home. She thrust into me. More pleasure. In. Out. In. Out. My body tightened. I was on the brink of oblivion. Harder. Faster. Harder. Faster.

I could almost reach my orgasm as it teased me from the ledge, and then I came. Waves of pleasure crashed over me, consuming me deep into a whirlpool of ecstasy.

"Oh. My. Fucking. Stars," I cried out. My heart pounded as I basked in the euphoria of an hour well spent.

"This is a good tub," I murmured to myself, sinking deeper into the warm embrace of the water. The jets continued their soothing massage as I let the remnants of my orgasm ebb away, leaving me completely relaxed and content. The candlelight flickered softly, and the scent of lavender lingered in the air. I took another sip of my wine, savoring the moment.

Yes, this was going to be a great week.

7
Ophelia

I woke up from the deepest sleep, momentarily forgetting where I was. Disoriented, I reached for my cell phone. It was 9:30 a.m. Absolute shock. I thought myself incapable of sleeping in. The morning sun danced brightly across the room, painting golden hues on the quaint bed and breakfast walls. I didn't want to leave the soft, billowy sensation beneath me. With a contented sigh, I sank back into the cloud-like bed. It felt like I was floating on a sea of marshmallows. The plush comforter draped me in a warm embrace, coaxing me to linger a little longer.

The haze of sleep finally lifted. A grin tugged at the corners of my lips as I stretched luxuriously, relishing the decadent indulgence of a lazy morning. I threw off the covers with renewed energy. The promise of adventure beckoned to me from beyond the coziness of bed. Another stretch, and I pulled open the drapes leading out to the balcony. The town looked like a movie set bathed in sunlight. The entire main street of Coral Cove was a beautiful sepia.

With a decisive nod, I decided to make the most of this unexpected, gorgeous day. The seaside breeze whispered through the open sliding door and tousled my hair in playful tendrils. A renewed sense of optimism filled me. I glanced at the woman in the mirror. There was a glow in her cheeks and a lightness in her heart. Somehow, she felt less familiar today. I stared into her eyes, and it was as if galaxies swirled, stars sparkled, and the moon's brightness was captured at the center. I blinked a few times, and the universe retreated. Still me.

As I stepped into the hallway, the scent of freshly brewed coffee lingered. I smiled and descended the creaky wooden stairs. The anticipation of the day added a skip to my step.

"Good morning, my dear," May, the owner of the B&B and restaurant, grinned. "Did you sleep well?"

"Good morning! Yes, that bed was a cloud. Thanks again for being so accommodating when I got in yesterday," I said.

"Oh, of course, dear. Is everything in the room satisfactory?" May asked.

"Everything is fantastic. That tub is something special. Thank you for leaving the candles. A relaxing bath was exactly what I needed to settle in."

"Oh, I am so happy you are enjoying yourself," May said. "Come, sit!" May brought over a cup and a menu. "Coffee?" she asked.

"Yes, please." I perused the menu. "I'll have the cheesy eggs scrambled but no sausage, please. Oh, and no onions."

"Of course. Would you like a side of toast?"

"Sourdough, please."

Strings of vibrant paper lanterns hung from the ceiling, casting a familiar warmth. Intricate paper cutouts adorned the walls, depicting scenes with dragons and blooming lotus flowers in celebration of the Mooncake Festival. The whimsical charm of the restaurant assured me I had stumbled onto a hidden gem. Near the entrance of the restaurant was a stack of menus. I jumped up to grab one. I couldn't help but smile at its content. It was a tantalizing mix of traditional Asian cuisine and special festival treats, each description more tempting than the last.

"Oh, you found our dinner menus," May said, returning with my food.

"My goodness, everything sounds delicious. I can't wait to have dinner here," I handed the menu to May.

"You're lucky to be here at such a special time. We have lots of Mooncake Festival additions. There's magic in the air," May said, dancing away smiling.

My phone rang, and I dug into my bag for it. "Hello?"

It was Melody. "Do you have the deposition for the Gallagar file?"

"Yes, my secretary should be able to get you whatever you need. Did something happen? Do I need to come back?"

"No, no, no. You're fine. I've got you, boo. Go relax and enjoy yourself."

"If you say so."

After breakfast, I explored town, eager to lose myself in the winding streets and hidden treasures. I remembered where I wanted my first stop to be. I had a craving for the scent of books and the hushed reverence of the bookstore. The bell dinged overhead as I opened the door. A magical hum buzzed from every corner inside.

"Hello! Welcome. Let me know if you need help finding anything," a woman behind the cash register said.

"Hi," I said. "Thank you so much." I didn't know where to begin.

The center of the store was a huge tree, shelves built into its makeshift trunk. Every part drew attention. Immediately, I moved to the young adult section. Their colorful covers always catch my eye. I picked up a book with a beautiful cover: *From A Youth, A Fountain Did Flow* by Miranda Levi. The book had an allure about it. In the center, behind the title, was a human heart that was both jarring and breathtaking.

"This looks good," I said. "Oh, it has a sequel, *The Sea Withdrew*." I grabbed the second novel and read the back. I glanced up from the book and yipped. The books slipped and crashed to the ground.

"I didn't mean to frighten you," a woman said.

The sight of her made my breath catch in my throat. She was bathed in golden light, radiating an aura of undeniable allure.

"I—I just didn't realize you were standing there," I stumbled over my words. "You were hidden in sunlight."

She smiled. "You're okay. Here, let me help you." She bent down and picked up the books I dropped.

There was an ethereal quality about this woman that set her apart. Her skin glowed warm and luminous, as if touched by the sun's rays itself. Even in the shadows, she glowed. Long, flowing locks of golden hair cascaded down her back in shimmering waves. Occasionally, it caught the light, casting a halo around her head. Her eyes, the color of molten gold, pierced through my soul. Every movement she made was a fluid, choreographed dance. The fabric of her golden dress clung to her curves, accentuating her body.

"Here you go," she handed me the two novels with a smile.

"Thank you," I said. I couldn't think of anything else to say. She lingered in silence. "I'm Ophelia."

"Ophelia," she repeated, rolling my name over her tongue. "A beautiful name for a beautiful woman."

The compliment sent a shiver down my spine. I couldn't tear my gaze away from her. There was an unexplained stirring inside of me. Every fiber of my being was drawn into this woman. It was a magnetic pull that left my head swirling.

"What's your name?" I asked finally.

"Hm?"

"I'm Ophelia, and you're?" I said.

"Oh," she paused and stared deep into my eyes. A flush of heat rose to my cheeks. My heart thumped. Thump. Thump. Thump.

"My name is Lillian."
Thump.
"Hello, Lillian."
The air around us was charged with electrifying energy, crackling with the power of the sun itself. The scent of new books, sandalwood, and mooncakes filled me with desire and awe. Time stood still as we locked in a silent exchange.

8
Lillian

We stood in a comfortable silence. I just looked at my love. Two and a half years is a long time to wait for air. I left the flower shop and went for a walk, sort of just wandering the streets. I stopped into a couple of cute shops, said hello to a couple of friendly faces, but the moment I saw the bookstore, I was drawn in. I had never read much, so I couldn't explain the allure. Except I can. Here we were, staring at each other. The love of my life was waiting for me in this little bookstore.

"Are you from here?"

"No," Ophelia said breathlessly. "I'm just a tourist. I got in last night from Chicago. You?"

"Chicago, huh. What do you do there?" I asked. She's moved since last I saw her. Although she didn't remember me after. She rarely does.

"I'm an attorney," Ophelia said.

"That makes sense," I said, thinking of all the ways she had no voice and of all the ways she's spent her human lives finding it again.

"What makes you say that?" Her smile made my knees quake.

"It's your essence. The way you carry yourself. I bet you're a boss in all aspects of your life." I bit my bottom lip.

Ophelia turned scarlet. She looked down at the floor. I had her intrigued. I felt the fabric of her sweater.

"I really like this jumper. Where did you get it?"

I didn't care. I needed a reason to touch her.

"Oh, I don't know? I think Costco, maybe," she pulled at her sweater, still flushed by my presence.

"Are you in town alone?" I asked.

She nodded, "I am. I needed a break from work. Suddenly, some time opened in my schedule, and here I am." She readjusted her hair. "What about you?"

"All alone," I admitted. "Lucky for me, I popped in here."

"What do you like to read?" Ophelia asked.

"Secret?"

"Always," she leaned in conspiratorially.

"I haven't read a book in years. I never really got the appeal," I grimaced.

Ophelia threw up her hands. "You had me until this very moment. I was ready to ask if you wanted to walk around town. But you hate books," she shook her head exaggeratedly.

"How was I to know that I'd meet an angel? Alone—in this beautiful town. I would have taken up reading years ago if I could only see the future," I said.

A smile played on her lips. "Can you name the last book you read?"

I made a show of thinking about it. "It had a red cover with a heart."

She tilted her head and looked down at her books. "No fair, you're cheating."

"The last cover I read. Did you mean, what was the last cover you read, Lillian? Right?" I winked.

"How about I make an exception?" Ophelia said.

"You'd do that for me?" I asked innocently.

"Two ladies, alone...together. I suppose just this one time." Her smile sent warmth through my chest.

"Can I buy those books for you?" I asked, reaching to take them from her.

She hesitated.

"Consider it an apology for startling you and not having picked up a book in ages," I said.

She sighed, exaggerating a roll of her eyes. "Since you made me squeal, I'll say thank you. That's very kind."

I'm going to make her do more than squeal. I'm going to make Ophelia scream my name. We took the books to the front.

"Did you find everything okay?" Lea asked.

"More than everything," I said. "I know I've been saying I'll pop in for ages, and I fail major."

"Haha, it's okay," Lea said with a chuckle.

"But for real, it's lovely. Everything Alex described and more," I said.

"Thank you!" Lea beamed. "I didn't realize it would take a pretty face to get you in here," she winked. "Are you in town for the Mooncake Festival?"

Ophelia and I exchanged glances.

"How did you know?" Ophelia asked.

Lea's eyes grew big. "Oh, wonderful! Here, I have a couple of mooncakes if you'd like."

"Thank you, Lea. That's so kind," I said.

"I hope you two have a lovely day," Lea said. "There's magic in the air. Enjoy some of that for me, too."

"We will," Ophelia said.

"Tell Alex I said hi," I waved goodbye. The heart of Coral Cove was lined with colorful storefronts hiding cozy cafes, which beckoned to us. It breathed the energy of the Mooncake Festival. We walked side by side. Our shoulders brushed one another. Ophelia moved with a subtle sway of her hips, oozing confidence and grace.

"I know typically, one of us should ask what the other does for a living. We would pore over everything we do to support ourselves, but life is short, and most of that doesn't matter. I want to know what makes you smile. I want to know what song you listen to when you're sad. I want to know everything about you," my words came out eager and breathless.

Ophelia's eyes sparkled. She took a deep breath, her body sort of shrinking on itself. As she let it out, all of her relaxed. "Winning makes me happy. I know that sounds conceited, but remember, I'm going for honest." She waited a beat, leaving an opening for me.

I smiled but remained quiet. She went on.

"As for a song, the context of why I'm sad changes which one I'd play. If it was a breakup or a shitty date, then I'd probably go with 'abcdefu' by Gayle. Or 'We Are Never Ever Getting Back Together' by Taylor Swift. But if it's just been a hard day, then it's probably something a bit more screamy."

"How beautifully interesting. The Swifty listens to screamy music," I said, unable to hide my smile. "Brilliant."

"Your turn," Ophelia said.

"Coral Cove is my happy place. When I'm sad, I listen to 'Drunk On The Moon' by Tom Waits. When I'm angry with the world, my go-to is 'Total Eclipse Of The Heart' by Bonnie Tyler."

"Oh, that's a good one," Ophelia hummed part of the song.

"Right? So good," I gestured to the pier, and she nodded. We started walking toward it. "I think it's your turn."

Ophelia scrunched her perfect little nose. "Do you rehearse what you'll say before you make a phone call?"

"Depends on who it's to," I said, thinking about the question a little more. "If it's to family, always. If it's anyone else, rarely."

"Same, oddly enough. Most people I know are the opposite. They never think with family but always get in their head about strangers," Ophelia said.

"Right? I don't care what a stranger thinks of me. But I care about my family. I'm afraid to disappoint them more than I already have." I regretted my words immediately. "I mean—"

"No, no, I get that. I'm a successful lawyer up for partner. But I'm still a disappointment. Unmarried and the lack of grandchildren for my parents to fawn over will be my downfall," she said.

"Haha, yes," I laughed. "Okay, I have one."

"Go for it," Ophelia clapped her hands.

"Tell me something you've always dreamed of doing," I said. "And it can't be something to do with your current job."

"I see you." We reached the pier and leaned over the edge, watching the water.

"I'd love to use one of those enormous telescopes. Do you know the one I'm talking about?" she asked.

"Oh yeah, like the Hale in San Francisco."

"Yes!" she radiated joy. "I think I was an astronomer in another life."

"No, but you've always loved the stars," I said without thinking.

She chuckled uncomfortably. "Why do you say that?"

I forced a laugh, "Jokes."

"Oh," she relaxed.

We lingered there, enjoying the salty air and the rhythmic sound of the waves. The sun was starting to dip toward the horizon, casting a golden glow over everything.

"Shall we continue our walk?" I asked.

"Yes, let's," Ophelia agreed, her smile brighter than the setting sun.

Dawning Desire

As we strolled along the pier, I couldn't help but feel that this time, maybe, just maybe, things would be different. The magic of Coral Cove was undeniable, and with Ophelia by my side, I was ready to believe in it again.

9
Ophelia

For a moment, Lillian spoke as though she's known me forever. Worse? I believed her.

"What about you?" I asked. "If you could live out a dream, what would it be?"

Lillian's smile is so kissable. She took my breath away. She smelled like freshly baked cookies. I want to lick her.

"Anything? I'd open a flower shop," she smiled uncomfortably.

"Flowers?"

"I enjoy growing things," Lillian said.

"Somehow, that suits you well," I couldn't help but smile. "What's your favorite flower?" I asked.

"Moonflower. They only emerge at night. They represent beauty and romance. The moonflower says I'm in love with you even through the darkness," she found my eyes, and somehow, I've never felt more seen than right now.

"Mine is the sunflower. They follow the sun and move to catch as many of its rays as possible. The sunflower says, I'm loyal, full of joy, and will always wait for you."

My stomach dropped. I'd never been so honest with someone before. Lillian slipped her fingers into mine.

We walked toward a bustling farmers market in the square. Vendors were selling a little bit of everything. The air was alive with the scent of freshly baked pastries and exotic spices mingling with the briny tang of the sea. Lillian picked up a fresh mooncake from a vendor's stall. She paid and pulled my hand, leading me to the side of the stall.

I locked eyes with Lillian as she brought the pastry to her lips. She took a slow, deliberate bite. A low hum of pleasure escaped her lips. She took another slow bite. Her lips were lightly covered with crumbs. I wanted to taste the sweet confection right off her mouth.

"You should try this," Lillian said in a husky voice. She handed me her partly eaten cake. I examined the cake, found her eyes, and took a bite. The crumbly cake fell apart in her hands. I reached forward to help her catch the pieces with a giggle.

"This is really good," I said, mumbling through my mouthful. The air crackled. An unspoken tension built between us. I wanted to kiss this woman more than I've wanted to do anything else.

I was bumped from behind by someone, breaking the moment. "Sorry," the person said, moving right by. I waved politely. Lillian and I moved through the farmer's market. There was a light skip to our walk.

I paused to look at some jewelry pieces. Lillian was glancing at something else, and I waved quietly to the woman in the stall.

"Hi," I whispered. "Could you wrap that up real quick?" I said, pointing to one of her pieces. I mouthed, "It's a gift," and pointed to Lillian.

She winked at me in acknowledgment and quietly wrapped the item. When Lillian wasn't looking, I slipped the woman some cash and took the gift.

"Thank you," I whispered.

"You're very welcome," she said with a smile. "She's going to love it."

As we continued our stroll, I held the small package behind my back, anticipation building. I couldn't wait to see the look on Lillian's face when she opened it.

We walked to a tucked away spot near the water, where the hustle and bustle of the market faded into a gentle hum.

"I have something for you," I said, finally revealing the gift.

Lillian's eyes widened in surprise. "For me?"

"Open it," I urged, handing her the wrapped package.

She carefully unwrapped the paper, revealing a delicate silver necklace with a small moonflower pendant. Her eyes sparkled.

"It's beautiful," she whispered. "Thank you."

"I saw it and thought of you," I said softly.

Lillian smiled, her eyes misty. She reached up to clasp the necklace around her neck, and I helped her fasten it. The pendant rested perfectly against her skin.

We stood there for a moment, taking in the beauty of the evening and the quiet connection between us. It felt like we were the only two people in the world. The air around us was charged with something electric, something magical.

"Do you believe in fate?" Lillian asked, her voice barely above a whisper.

"I think I do now," I replied, looking into her eyes.

In that moment, everything was perfect.

10
Lillian

We continued to explore Coral Cove. I drew Ophelia into a secluded alleyway, seeking a gentle moment of privacy.

"May I take your picture?" I asked, pulling out my phone. "I never want to forget this day."

"Me either," Ophelia said, taking a step backward. "How's this?"

"You're perfect." I took a photo of her and smiled. "Thank you."

"My turn?" she pulled her phone from her pocket and looked at me with big puppy dog eyes.

I nodded. "Of course."

Ophelia snapped a photo.

"Why astronomy?" I asked, thinking back to our earlier conversation. "You said a telescope."

Ophelia was thoughtful for a moment. "Well, according to legend, there was a hermit named Orion who lived alone on a distant island, spending his nights hunting and his days sleeping. Little did he know, he had a celestial admirer, Artemis, the moon goddess. She drove her horses and the moon across the sky every night.

Despite being forbidden to mingle with mortals, Artemis fell in love with Orion." Ophelia arched a brow.

"Intrigue," I made an O with my lips.

"Breaking all the rules made by the divine, Artemis went to Earth, and their forbidden romance flourished. That is, until her brother Apollo found them and turned them in to Zeus. So enraged at the betrayal, Zeus sent a giant scorpion to kill Orion. After a fierce battle, Orion succumbed to the scorpion's sting."

"What happened?" I asked.

"Heartbroken, Artemis flung the scorpion into the sky, where it became Scorpius. She immortalized her lover Orion as a constellation on the opposite side of the sky, ensuring the scorpion would never get Orion again," she finished.

"It's such a sad story, though. Two people who could never really be together because the gods didn't recognize true love," I looked away from her.

"You're not wrong. I think most of us aren't lucky enough to find our one true love. They got to be together, even if it was only for a short while," Ophelia said.

I reached for her hand and slipped my fingers between hers. I trailed my fingers along Ophelia's jawline using a feather-light touch with the other. "You are something special, Ophelia."

A soft gasp escaped her lips. My heart raced, thudding so loudly I feared it might leave my body. A large multi-colored maple tree cast dappled shadows on her skin. I moved my mouth closer to hers. I licked my lips.

She leaned into my touch. Her body seemed to hum with desire. Our lips met in a searing kiss, a collision of passion and longing melting me into her embrace. Her hands tangled in my hair. Our tongues danced in a primal rhythm. Time stood still. We slowly lost ourselves in each other. She pulled me into her. I pressed my body against hers in a fevered embrace. My hands traced the curves of her spine, and I pulled her closer. Her hands moved down my neck, leaving a hot trail where her skin met mine.

Suddenly, Ophelia pulled back. "What am I doing?" she said hurriedly. She took a step away. "I'm sorry." She rushed out of the alleyway and back to the street.

11
Ophelia

I needed a moment alone to think. Sure, I've experimented with women in the past, but nothing has ever felt this intense or fast with anyone. Intensity isn't something I've experienced outside of the courtroom. Crossing the street, I jogged down to the water. It scared me. I just met this woman a few hours ago, and it's like I've known her my whole life. To be fair, I've spent less time with someone I'd dated for two or even three full weeks than I have with Lillian today. That means something.

A twinge of guilt hit me. I just ditched her back there and ran. God knows what she must be thinking about me. I rubbed my eyes and ran my fingers through my hair. I took three deep breaths. The two of us were lost in a world of sensation and pleasure. She was intoxicating.

Oh, my gods, what am I doing? I turned around and walked back. When I reached the alley, I said, "I hope I haven't killed the moment." But I didn't see Lillian anywhere. I walked further down the dark and quiet space to the maple tree at the end, wondering if there was another exit or a corner she was hiding behind. Instead, I found a courtyard. It was simple and somehow still elegant. There were doors to buildings, but they seemed more like service entrances than front doors. Standing in the middle was Lillian.

"Are you okay?" she asked.

"I am so sorry for taking off like that. I—"

Lillian raised her finger to my mouth. "Don't apologize. I'm just glad you're back." She smiled that cheeky grin that drew me to her in the first place.

"Why do I feel like I've known you forever?" I asked.

"Maybe you have," Lillian smiled. "Do you want to come back to mine?" she asked.

"No," I said.

Lillian's whole body sank in disappointment.

"No, wait. I mean, no, I think we should go back to mine."

"Oh," Lillian perked up. "My place is just up the road a bit."

"Mine has a jetted tub," I said.

"Your place sounds perfect," Lillian reached for my hand, and I let her lead us out of the alley back toward the main street.

Inside, Lillian took a self-guided tour of the space. "This is extremely cute," she said, disappearing into the tiny kitchen. Standing at the foot of the bed, I glanced around, looking for anything that might be embarrassing. Thankfully, someone came and made the bed. My wine glass from the night before was gone.

Lillian came back with two glasses of wine. "I found a half-opened bottle on the counter. I hope it was yours," she chuckled.

We locked eyes, and my stomach flip-flopped nervously. I sipped my wine. "Mmm, it's just as good as the night before."

Lillian took a sip, "Oh, it really is delightful."

"I got it to help me relax and get out of my head," I said.

"Gods, I love those paintings. They fit the esthetic perfectly," Lillian said. A smile played on her lips.

"I agree. Love them."

"What's through there?" Lillian pointed to the sliding glass door.

"Go look. It's a beautiful balcony."

She opened the door and stepped out. I followed closely behind.

"Oh, how perfect. Look, there's Main Street if you look over there," Lillian pointed. "That's my flower shop over there." There were a lot of people mingling outside, looking at the sky.

My phone rang. It was Melody.

"Do you need to get that?" Lillian asked.

I clicked it to silent. "Nothing is more important than now."

She smiled and leaned into me.

"The lunar eclipse must be soon," I said. "I'd almost forgotten about it altogether."

"I didn't," she said with a devious smile.

The wind kicked up, and the smell of Chinese food wafted from the Golden Chopsticks. I inhaled deeply.

"Now I want Chinese food," Lillian chuckled.

"Same! But there's something I want a little more right now." I can't believe I just said that. I laced my fingers with Lillian's and pulled her back inside. I took her glass of wine and set it on the dresser. I pulled her into me, and we fell sideways onto the bed. Lillian moaned gently as we landed.

With a shared urgency, our mouths found one another. I shed my inhibitions and slipped my fingers under her shirt. Feeling her stomach, her hips, her back. Lillian pulled me closer to her, removing any space between us. She slipped a leg between mine and moved it gently against my heat. A moan slipped from me, and Lillian bit my lip. She slipped her hands under my shirt, removing it.

"You're wearing too many clothes."

I pulled her shirt off, too, "Much better."

Lillian kissed my neck down my collarbone. She slipped a hand behind me, freeing me from my bra. Slowly, she pulled back from me, taking me in. Thirsty for more. She tossed her own to the floor with mine in a tangle of fabric.

I traced the lines of her skin, her breasts, and her belly button. She reached for me, pulling me closer. Skin against skin, we explored each other with a fervor born of desire. Her mouth found my breast, and she slipped her hands into my pants, pulling me close to her. I moaned with pleasure. Our bodies danced in harmony as we chased the edge of oblivion. Encouraged by my response, she continued her exploration, trailing kisses down the curve of my stomach.

With gentle hands, I traced the curves of her body, memorizing every dip and rise with a reverent touch. I marveled at the smoothness of her skin, the delicate arch of her neck, and the supple roundness of her breasts. Lillian's skin glowed with an otherworldly radiance. Her golden eyes smoldered, sending a shiver of anticipation down my spine. Lillian maneuvered me to my back and climbed on top of me. She unzipped my jeans, slipping them off me.

I arched my back, a silent plea for more. Lillian's lips and tongue dipped lower, tracing the path to my most intimate core.

"You're already slick with desire," her voice was guttural. With a low growl of hunger, Lillian buried her face between my thighs. Slow at first but quickly, a fervor born of longing grew. I gasped, sucking in a breath at the sudden pleasure. I never understood what the big deal was before. The idea was sexy, but it was always just okay. None of it ever felt like this. Nothing has ever felt this good.

Lillian licked and teased me, exploring every inch of me with skillful precision. I writhed beneath her touch. My hands clutched at the blanket beneath me as waves of pleasure washed over me.

"I'm going to make you squirt, baby," Lilian said.

"I've never done that," I said, realizing there's a lot about sex I haven't learned.

"You will, and I will bathe in your delectable taste," Lilian said. I had no words. She returned to my middle and continued her mission.

My body was a symphony of sensations. Every nerve ending was on fire with the exquisite pleasure she bestowed on me. The overwhelming need to explode built within me. Her mouth on me, she slipped two fingers inside of my pussy. She gently massaged my insides with a come-hither motion.

"Oh, my stars. What are you doing," I couldn't keep my eyes open.

"Is this okay?" she asked.

"My gods above, don't stop. Don't stop. Don't stop!" Fire erupted inside of me. An explosion behind my eyes and in my cunt radiating through my body. Nothing has ever felt so good.

"Fuuuuuuuuuck—oh, for the love of everything holy, my gods above," I cried out, unable to stop moaning. The climax of a lifetime. Lillian slowly released me. She kissed up my body and found my mouth. I savored the taste of myself on her lips, sweet and intoxicating. Her tongue gently massaged mine in a similar pattern she did with my pussy.

Cheers erupted outside. The start of the eclipse was happening.

"My body is like electrified Jell-O," I gasped, riding a wave of pleasure. "What did you do to me?"

"Oh, I'm not done yet." Lillian redoubled her efforts, spreading my legs further apart. She flicked her tongue inside of me while circling my clit with her fingers this time. Her tongue slipped in and out of me. Lillian savored every last drop as though she was a woman dying of dehydration, and my pussy was the first drink of water she'd had in days.

With a cry that echoed out into the streets, I shattered into a million sparkling fragments of pleasure, my body arching in a primal release.

"Lillian," I cried out.

The second orgasm pulsed through my body, but she did not let up. She continued to lavish her attention on me, riding out the waves of my climax with tender care. She lapped at my clit gently, coaxing every tremor of pleasure from my quivering body.

"Ooooh, Lillian," I moaned again.

She was relentless. The third wave of passion started to course through my body. I grabbed the headboard. Holding on for dear life. Everything went white. A veil lifted, and suddenly, I was everywhere and nowhere. My consciousness flickered and flashed, and whiteness was all I could see. In a sinking instant, I was slammed back into my body.

"Tai-Yang!" I screamed.

The name burst out of me, unbidden, as if torn from the depths of my soul. My body trembled with the aftershocks of pleasure, and I lay there, gasping for breath. Lillian's eyes widened at the name, her expression shifting from surprise to something deeper, something ancient and knowing.

Lillian leaned over me, her golden eyes locking onto mine. "You remember," she whispered, her voice a mixture of awe and reverence.

A flood of memories washed over me, disjointed and fleeting but unmistakably real. Lives lived, loves lost, and a connection that transcended time and space. I looked at Lillian—no, Tai-Yang— and everything fell into place.

"I remember," I said, my voice trembling. "It's you. It's always been you."

She smiled, a radiantly, lighting up the room. I pulled her close, our foreheads touching as we shared this moment of rediscovery.

12
Tai-Yang

"You're back, my love," I said, crawling back up her body. Luna's eyes welled with tears. I pulled her into an embrace, both of us crying silently at the overwhelming emotions. The moon goddess slowly came back to herself. Luna's body still trembling with the aftershocks of pleasure. Clarity lifted the thick veil of punishment she'd been living under.

Luna gazed up at me, her eyes filled with awe, love, and a deep-seated longing that tugged at my heart. I brushed a strand of hair away from her cheek. It was Ophelia's face, but my Luna was there now. I stroked her, wiping away her tears.

"My love," Luna whispered, her voice barely above a breath. A swell of emotion threatened to pour out of me. I traced her jawline with a trembling finger, providing her encouragement and assurance.

"This was real?" Luna asked.

"Yes, my love. And we were together," I said.

"It's been so long," her voice caught in her throat. The weight of nearly thirty years of longing and separation crashed over her in a tidal wave of emotion. I was familiar with this emotion, and I've seen it dozens of times. Lifetime after lifetime.

"Why has it been so long?" Luna asked.

"Because in this life, you're a very busy woman who doesn't take time for herself," I offered. "You rarely make it here within the twelve hours we have. There was one time, five years ago. You faded before my eyes," I said, grimacing at the memory.

"I remember. Ophelia couldn't explain how she'd gotten here. It was a doozy. But she'd felt drawn to this place ever since," Luna said, remembering.

Unable to hold back any longer, I sought the moon goddess' lips in a hungry, desperate kiss. It was a kiss filled with years of pain, patience, and love transcending time and space. When we broke apart, our foreheads remained pressed against each other as we struggled to catch our breaths. Luna traced my lips with her thumb, her eyes searching for the right words. But there were none. In the depths of Ophelia's eyes, I saw my Luna. I saw only love—pure, unadulterated, and unwavering love.

"I waited for you," I whispered.

"And I for you," Luna replied, her voice trembling with emotion. "Thirty years is an eternity without you."

"We're almost there, my love," I said. "It's been over 9,000 years. Our punishment is almost done. Only a few more lifetimes, and we're free," I stroked her hair. "We can be together always."

"I love you," Luna said, tears falling. "I can't believe you would do this for me."

Dawning Desire

"I'm doing this for us. I love you too, my moon."

We lay together in silence for a time. The Mooncake Festival buzzed to a gentle level of commotion. Waves and the soft breeze filled its space. In each other's arms, we found sanctuary where time stood still, and our love burned brighter than the sun and moon combined.

As Luna lay in my arms, a renewed passion stirred within me. Luna gazed up at me. Her fingertips traced the contours of my face with gentle strokes. "My love," she whispered. Her eyes sparkled with desire.

I leaned over to capture her lips in a searing kiss. It was a kiss filled with a hunger born of love and longing, a silent vow of devotion and desire. Our bodies moved together, hands roaming freely over one another. Re-exploring every inch with a newfound sense of urgency.

"I want to remember everything," Luna breathed against my lips, her voice a soft plea.

13
Luna

It was my turn. I trailed kisses down Tai-Yang's neck and collarbone. I savored the taste of her skin, nipping and sucking at the sensitive flesh, eliciting a low involuntary moan of pleasure from her lips. My beautiful sun was slick with anticipation. Slowly, I spread her legs. She offered herself to me completely.

I ran a finger down her body, tracing lines, guiding myself lower until my lips hovered just above her most intimate core. Tai-Yang sighed softly. I pressed my lips to her folds, consuming her. Claiming her as my own. I teased her, exploring with languid strokes of my tongue. Tai-Yang squirmed beneath me, moaning. Her breathing became more ragged, her body trembling with release. Her hips arched, urging me closer.

With a longing that bordered on desperation, I licked and sucked her, flicking my tongue in a swirling rhythm that drove Tai-Yang wild with need. A guttural cry of pleasure escaped her lips. I rolled her to the side and positioned my pussy to her lips while still having access to hers. Lazy style. Her mouth hungrily found my wet heat.

Tai-Yang slipped her fingers inside of me while devouring my pleasure center.

I slipped three fingers inside of Tai-Yang. Her walls clenched around me, pulsating in response. My eyes closed as if a planet went supernova. I was rocketed with bliss. Tai-Yang began to tremble, and I knew she was in the throes of a powerful orgasm, too. Love filled me wholly.

Our bodies moved in perfect harmony, a dance of passion and desire. Every touch, every kiss, every moan was a testament to the love we shared. As we reached the pinnacle of our pleasure, the world around us seemed to fade away, leaving only the two of us, united in a moment of pure ecstasy.

When the waves of our orgasms finally subsided, we lay entwined, our breaths mingling in the cool night air. The sounds of the Mooncake Festival drifted up from the streets below, a gentle reminder of the world beyond our sanctuary. But for now, we were content to remain in our bubble, basking in the afterglow of our lovemaking.

"I love you," I whispered, my voice filled with the depth of my feelings.

"I love you too," Tai-Yang replied, her eyes shining with emotion. "Always."

We held each other close, knowing that our love was eternal, transcending time and space.

14
Tai-Yang

Luna brought me to the brink of ecstasy and beyond. Our bodies glistened with sweat as we lay entwined in a tangle of limbs and heavy breaths. Our hearts pounded in unison.

"I'm so happy you found me," Luna said.

"Baby, this is destiny. I will find you in every lifetime across this universe. I have been here for every single eclipse over Coral Cove. I will continue to be here until this curse is lifted," I said, kissing her forehead.

"We only get these twelve hours of clarity. Can we go for a walk? Tell me what you've been doing since my last life?" Luna suggested.

We got up and dug through the clothing strewn all over the room until we both had enough to venture back downstairs and into the town. My heart was heavy with the impending loss of her memory again. I pushed that thought aside, determined to make the most of the time we had left. Hand in hand, we made our way back out into the streets of Coral Cove.

I caught Luna up on the state of the gods and how I had spent the days since I had seen her last. In her most recent life, Luna was Melvin, a middle-school teacher. After we met in Coral Cove, Luna lost her memories again, and I took on the role of Margaret. Melvin and I married and lived together until he passed, a little over thirty years ago. I mourned his passing but knew Luna would return reincarnated as someone new. Just as she always did.

Luna was Spencer before Melvin and Gertrude before that. Gertrude was an interesting one. She was an immigrant from Germany, and I hadn't learned German yet. We spoke the language of love, though.

"Gertrude was wonderful," Luna said with fondness. In these twelve hours, Luna remembered all her reincarnations.

"Ich liebe dich noch immer," Luna said.

"I love you too," I said. "I think Ophelia and I will get along just fine."

"Oh yeah? How are you going to woo me?" Luna asked.

"I don't need to. I had Ophelia fully seduced," I grinned.

Luna laid her head on my shoulder as we continued walking down the streets, our hands still intertwined, enjoying one another for every single moment we could.

Eventually, we looped Main Street twice and found ourselves back at the Golden Chopsticks. There was a coziness to the restaurant that called to us both. We settled at a private table by the window. The soft glow of candlelight cast a romantic ambiance over the moment. I reached across the table and entwined my fingers with Luna's.

She squeezed my hand, "Fate has brought us together again, my love."

"I'll never leave your side," I said. We placed our order, never looking away from each other. Soon, our wonton soup, spring rolls, stir-fried noodles, and Peking duck were served. Between bites, we exchanged soft whispers and gentle caresses. Our love for each other was palpable in the air.

"Do you two love birds need anything else?" May asked.

Luna glanced up this time. "Oh, hello again. Everything was lovely," Luna said.

"Oh yes, delicious," I said.

"Here are a couple of mooncakes, on the house," May said, setting them on the table before slipping away.

"Mooncake?" I asked, handing her one.

"I don't mind if I do," Luna smiled.

"This place is an absolute gem," I said.

"Will you keep bringing me here? Even after a thousand years? The magic of the place fills me with such joy," Luna said.

"I don't know if it's the town or if it's just because you're here. But the answer is yes."

After dinner, we strolled, hand in hand, along the moonlit beach. The waves crashed on the shore in a soothing rhythm. We shared laughter, stories, and dreams as if we had all the time in the world. But the hours slipped by quickly. We returned to the bed and breakfast.

We settled back into bed, and I pulled Luna close, wrapping her in a cocoon of warmth and love. We lay together for a long moment, savoring the feeling of being in each other's arms.

"I wish we had more time," Luna said.

"Me too," I answered, barely above a whisper. I traced the outline of her body with my finger, listening to the melody of her breath, not speaking. Simply feeling her essence and being.

"I love you, Tai-Yang," she whispered.

"I love you too, my sweet Luna."

As we drifted closer and closer to sleep, our bodies entwined, and our hearts beat as one. We knew this time was precious and fleeting. But we had love and passion on our side. In the morning, Luna would once again be Ophelia. She would forget the past twelve hours. For now, we were not just goddesses of the moon and the sun—we were soulmates destined to be together for all time.

"Tai Yang?" she asked.

"Yes, my love."

"Promise you will be here with me in the morning," Luna said.

"Always," I whispered.

"Luna?" I said.

"Yeah?"

"Don't forget me, okay?" I asked, even though I knew it could not be so. It was an impossibility.

Luna held me tighter. "Never," she whispered back.

As we lay together in the soft light of the early morning, I held onto Luna, savoring every moment. The love we shared was a beacon of hope, a promise that no matter how many lifetimes passed, we would always find our way back to each other.

Eventually, sleep claimed us both, and as I drifted off, I whispered one final vow to the moon and the stars above, "Until the end of time, my love."

And in the stillness of the dawn, under the watchful eyes of the cosmos, two souls found their peace, bound together by a love that could never be broken.

If you like my Coral Cove Series, be sure to check out the first book in the Tarot Fantasy series:

The Devil's Temptations

When Dorothea steps into The Arcane Room, a quaint new-age shop, she doesn't expect her life to change forever. Drawn to the captivating Ms. Vesper and the promise of a magical experience, Dorothea finds herself in a world where tarot cards reveal one's deepest desires. Pulled into a tantalizing simulation, she meets Lucian, a figure of raw, dangerous allure. Together, they explore the depths of her fantasies, pushing boundaries and igniting passions she never knew existed.

As Dorothea learns to let go of her fears and embrace her true self, she discovers that real magic lies in courage and love. With Lucian by her side, she faces challenges that transform her from a timid woman into an empowered heroine ready to take on the world.

Perfect for fans of: Steamy romances, magical realism, and stories of self-discovery and empowerment. If you enjoy the blend of passion and mysticism, "The Devil's Temptation" will captivate your heart and soul.

<u>Trope Highlights</u>
Virgin Heroine
Magical Realism
Forbidden Romance
Second Chance at Love
Self-Discovery and Empowerment

Additional Books by Rainbow Quartz Publishing

Jax Wilder

Coral Cove Series
Sleighed by Love
Harvesting Love
Dawning Desire
Knead You Now – August 2024
Love Rewound – September 2024
Haunted by Her – September 2024
Perfect Lover Spell – October 2024

Tarot Fantasies Series
The Devil's Temptations – August 2024
Strength of the Beast – August 2024
Death's Embrace – August 2024
Hanged Passions – September 2024
Swords of Sorrow – September 2024

Lorelai Hamilton
Find Your Bliss
Teenage Witch's Grimoire
Tarot Reflection Journal
Tarot Refection Journal Coloring The Tarot
The Eclectic Witch's Grimoire
Dream Journal
Teenage Tarot
Tarot Tales and Magic Spells
Arcane In Verse

Miranda Levi
From A Youth A Fountain Did Flow
The Sea Withdrew
A Tear In Time
Mo(ther) Na(ture)
In Orion's Hands

Jackson Anhalt
From The 911 Files

Lorelai Hamilton
Find Your Bliss
Teenage Witch's Grimoire
Tarot Reflection Journal
Tarot Refection Journal Coloring The Tarot
The Eclectic Witch's Grimoire
Dream Journal
Teenage Tarot
Tarot Tales and Magic Spells
Arcane In Verse

Isla Watts
A Fairy Bad Day
Surprise! You're a Vampire
Gorgeous, Gorgeous, Gorgons

Jax Wilder

Rose Dawson's Book Journals

Acknowledgments

I am deeply grateful for the unwavering support and encouragement from my family and friends throughout this writing journey. Their belief in my abilities and their patience during the long hours of solitude have been my greatest source of strength.

Furthermore, I extend my sincere gratitude to my amazing beta readers. A special thank you goes out to Larissa, Kaytie, and Angie. Your time and thoughts are always invaluable.

About the Author

Jax Wilder is a passionate romance author hailing from a charming small town nestled in the picturesque Pacific Northwest. With a heart full of love and an unyielding belief in the power of happily ever afters, Jax weaves enchanting tales of love and connection that leave readers captivated.

In her own life, Jax is happily married to her soulmate, Daylin, whose unwavering support and love inspire her every day. They share their cozy home with two lovable Great Danes, Biscuit and Milly, who add an extra layer of joy to their lives. When she's not lost in the world of romance fiction, Jax enjoys exploring the beauty of the Pacific Northwest, savoring long walks with her beloved dogs, and discovering the hidden gems of her small town.

Jax's novels are a reflection of her commitment to celebrating the magic of love, and her characters' journeys mirror the warmth and happiness she has found in her own life. Join her on the enchanting journey of love, passion, and enduring connection through her heartfelt romance novels.